Bull's Eye

DISCARD

Bull's Eye

Sarah N. Harvey

Orca soundings

Orca Book Publishers

Library and Archives Canada Cataloguing in Publication

Harvey, Sarah N., 1950-

Bull's-Eye / written by Sarah N. Harvey.
(Orca soundings)

ISBN 978-1-55143-681-4 (bound)
ISBN 978-1-55143-679-1 (pbk.)

I. Title. II. Series.

PS8615.A764B84 2007   jC813'.6   C2007-902429-7

Summary: After the death of her aunt, Emily finds that her life has been a lie
and she has to search for the truth about where she came from and who she is.

First published in the United States, 2007
Library of Congress Control Number: 2007926444

Orca Book Publishers gratefully acknowledges the support for its publishing
programs provided by the following agencies: the Government of Canada
through the Book Publishing Industry Development Program and the Canada
Council for the Arts, and the Province of British Columbia through the BC
Arts Council and the Book Publishing Tax Credit.

Cover design: Teresa Bubela
Cover photography: Maxx Images
Author photo: Dayle Sutherland

Orca Book Publishers   Orca Book Publishers
PO Box 5626 Station B   PO Box 468
Victoria, BC Canada   Custer, WA USA
V8R 6S4   98240-0468

www.orcabook.com
Printed and bound in Canada.
Printed on 100% PCW recycled paper.

010 09 08 07 • 5 4 3 2 1

To Brian
Brother, friend, cheerleader

Acknowledgments

My sincere thanks to Mark Sieben of the British Columbia Ministry of Children and Family Development who patiently answered my questions about the child welfare system in BC, and to Dave Johnson of the John Howard Society of British Columbia, who provided valuable insight into the challenges of dealing with juveniles in the justice system. Thanks also to Andrew McWhinnie, whose passion for restorative justice pointed me in the right direction. Any mistakes are entirely my own and not the fault of these intelligent and generous men.

Thanks also to everyone at Orca, especially Andrew Wooldridge—artful editor, worthy Ping-Pong opponent and expert rodent-wrangler.

Chapter One

I'm the only one home when the UPS guy delivers the package that blows up my life. No, it isn't a letter bomb sent to my mother by a disgruntled client, but it might as well be. A hand grenade with the pin already pulled would do less damage than what is in the plain cardboard box addressed to my mother, Ms. Sandra Bell. I'm home alone because I have strep throat. My mom has taken a break from slaving over other people's tax returns to go and get me some Ben & Jerry's Jamaican Me Crazy sorbet to soothe my throat.

Mom has been acting pretty weird ever since her younger sister Donna died. Lots of crying and long solitary walks on the beach. I can't even get her to play Scrabble, which is her all-time favorite game. Aunt Donna was my mom's only living relative, so Mom was pretty choked when Donna's sponsor called from Toronto to say that Donna was dead. By her own hand, as they say. She had gobbled a bottle of Valium and chased it with an entire bottle of Johnnie Walker. Very effective. Clearly not a cry for help, although there had been plenty of those over the years. My mom was always flying to Toronto to bail Donna out of one mess or another. She's just come back from her final trip. She brought Donna's ashes back in a Baggie. Apparently the plan is to scatter them over English Bay. That'll be fun.

I didn't really know Aunt Donna. She came to Victoria to see us once when I was about six. Since I never went to Toronto with my mom, I have no idea what my aunt was like. Other than messed up, I mean. It sounded to me like Donna's death was the most organized thing she ever did.

I get so bored waiting for Mom to come back that I consider opening the package. I could have a peek inside and seal it up again before she gets home. In the end, I'm too lazy to get up and find the box cutter. Besides, I'm my mother's daughter: neat, hardworking, well-organized, thoughtful. When she finally comes back from the store, I'm sitting at the kitchen table, staring into space, chewing on a hangnail.

"Feeling better, honey?" she says. "Ready for some sorbet?" She places the back of her hand against my forehead for a moment. She smiles. "Temperature's down. That's good."

"A package came for you. It's in the living room," I say.

"A package?"

"Yeah. You know, like a box. Maybe

someone forgot to file his taxes for, like, ten years."

Usually my mom laughs at my feeble accountant jokes. Not this time. She puts the sorbet on the counter and walks into the living room without a word. When she comes back to the kitchen, she's carrying the box and her hands are shaking. She puts the box on the table in front of me and backs away from it. Maybe it really is a bomb.

"Open it, Emily," she says. "It's for you." Her voice is shaking too, and her normally rosy cheeks are ashen. Beads of sweat form along her upper lip. When she has a hot flash, her face gets really red, so this is something else.

"But it's addressed to you," I say.

"I know," she replies. "But it's for you. From Donna. In her note…"

She swipes at her tears and continues.

"The note Donna left—her suicide note— she wanted you to have this. I addressed it to myself so you wouldn't open it without me."

"Okay," I say. It feels all kinds of creepy, but let's face it: Aunt Donna had been a bit of a wack job. "Can I have a knife—and some sorbet? Before it melts? My throat's killing me."

Mom hands me the box cutter from the junk drawer. While she scoops sorbet into my favorite blue bowl, I slit the tape on the box. I don't know what I'm expecting to find—vintage clothes, cool shoes, funky jewelry? No such luck. The first thing I see is a high school annual from the school Mom and Donna went to in Vancouver. I set it aside and dig a little deeper. Underneath the annual are three large brown envelopes. The first has my mom's name written on it in green felt pen. The second is decorated with a curly letter *K*. The third says *Emily*. Emily? That's so weird. My heart flutter-kicks. Maybe Aunt Donna has left me a bunch of money. I break the seal on the envelope with my name on it and dump the contents on the table. It's not money. It's letters. A lot of letters.

I move on to the envelope marked *Sandra*. More letters. I hand them to my mom, but she shakes her head and says, "They're for you." In the envelope marked *K* are even more letters. I dig a little further. In the bottom of the box is a small, pink, crocheted blanket. As I pull it out and hang it over the back of a chair, I hear my mom inhale sharply, but she says nothing.

I pick up one of the letters from the *Emily* envelope and start reading. It's a birthday card. *Now you are Two*! There are sixteen others, all from Aunt Donna, all telling me how wonderful I am and how much she misses me. I wonder why she never sent any of them, but that was Aunt Donna. Letters unsent. Phone calls unreturned. Brain unused. The Sandra letters are from my mom to Donna, telling her how wonderful I am and how lucky she is to have me. The letters from K tell Donna how wonderful *she* is and how lucky he (or she) is to have her. It's a whole world of wonderfulness. I feel queasy. I had no idea Aunt Donna even knew when my birthday was. My mom has never mentioned that she sent her sister weekly updates on my unbelievable adorableness. And who the hell is K?

I turn the box upside down to make sure I haven't missed anything. A photo flutters out and lands on the carpet facedown. There's a date scrawled on the back—*Feb 15, 1989*. Three weeks before I was born. I turn it over. My mother and Aunt Donna are standing in front of the Sylvia Hotel in Vancouver's West End. I recognize it from all the times my mom and I have stayed there. In the photograph, Aunt Donna is very, very pregnant. My mother is not. I look up at my mom and she is crying silently, with her hand over her mouth. I just make it to the bathroom before I lose my breakfast, my lunch and my mind. I don't want sorbet anymore.

Chapter Two

When I finally come out of the bathroom, Mom—or whoever she is—is sitting at the kitchen table. The pink blanket is on her lap and she is staring at the photograph. My dish of sorbet is still sitting on the counter. Suddenly I crave the simple cold sweetness on my tongue. I stand silently, spooning the melted goop into my mouth. I finish off what's in the bowl and get the container out of the freezer and keep eating. It's easier than talking. And I figure the ball's in her court. No way am I starting this conversation.

"She made this for you, you know," she says. She strokes the blanket. "She was so young—your age. Can you imagine?"

I laugh. It comes out more like a seal's bark. Harsh and loud. I can't imagine anything at the moment, other than getting away from her and her lies.

I was nine when she told me I was a sperm-donor baby. Up until then I hadn't worried too much about not having a dad. I kind of wondered what had happened to mine, but lots of my friends had no dads. Vanessa's was dead, Rory's took off when Rory was little, Jason's was in jail. No biggie. My mom's best friends, Richard and Chris, were always around to do guy stuff with me. They would shoot hoops, fix my bike, order pizza, go to Daughter 'n' Dad Day at school. I wasn't suffering. But when I was eight I started bugging Mom nonstop to tell me about my dad. For some reason I got it into my head that he was a millionaire who had died in a tragic ballooning accident. When I turned nine, she took me out for burgers at Duck Soup, my favorite diner. She told me all about sperm banks and donors. She told me how she had wanted a baby so badly and how she had planned everything and how great it all was. She said my dad was a really smart, super-healthy medical student. She also said that when I was eighteen I could register somewhere and maybe find him and any half-siblings I might have. I was, like, yuck! No thanks. For years after that I thought sex involved plastic cups. I never talk to Mom about it. It still grosses me out.

"So the whole sperm-donor story was crap?" I say. "All that stuff about wanting a baby so much but not having a partner, and planning, and choosing the best donor? All total bullshit?"

"No," she says slowly. "Not all of it. I didn't have a partner. And I did want a baby very much, but I didn't plan on Donna getting pregnant. I didn't plan on adopting you. That just happened."

"Yeah, right." I snort and some sorbet goes up my nose. It feels okay. Very cooling. "So why make up the lame-ass sperm-donor story? Why not just—here's an original idea—tell me the truth? I've spent seventeen years listening to 'The truth is always the right choice' and 'Mutual trust is the cornerstone of successful relationships.' Do you really believe any of that shit, Mom? Or should I say…Aunt Sandra?"

Mom looks up from the photograph and glares at me. For a moment a spark flares in her eyes, but it is instantly flooded by her tears.

"Don't call me that, Emily. Donna gave birth to you but I'm still your mother. Legally, emotionally—"

"Just not biologically," I interrupt. "You forgot that part. And what about that other thing—the part about who my dad was? Still going to stick with the sperm-donor story? 'Cause I'm not buyin' it anymore."

"I know you're angry and hurt, Emily. I understand. Just let me explain. Please."

I look at her. Her hair is a mess, she has chewed off her lipstick, and her mascara has run. I'm sure I look like hell too. Part of me wants to climb into her lap and burrow my head into her shoulder like I did when I was little. Part of me wants to run out the back door. And a tiny evil part wants to nick her with the box cutter. Nothing serious. Just a little friendly bloodletting.

I settle for boosting myself up onto the counter and kicking my heels into the cupboards, which I know she hates. She gets up, fills a glass with water and sits down again, smoothing the blanket over her knees. She picks up the picture and stares at it.

"Donna was born when I was eleven. Unplanned but welcome—your grandmother's precious menopause baby. I went away to university when she was seven. I only saw her once or twice a year after that, but your nana kept me posted. She would tell me how pretty Donna was, how cute it was that she had a boyfriend when she was twelve, how Donna sewed all the latest styles on her little pink sewing machine. When Donna was about fifteen, Nana stopped boasting about her. All she ever said was that Donna was moody. I found out later that Donna was drinking a lot and cutting classes. That she had a lot of boyfriends—mostly older guys. When she was seventeen, in her last year at Northwood, she called me. I was working in Calgary. She told me she was pregnant. She was too far along for an abortion and she wanted to get away from Mom. She had quit school, and she asked if she could come and stay with me until she had the baby. She was planning on giving it up for adoption."

Mom stops for a moment and picks up her glass. The water slops onto the placemat as she raises the glass to her mouth.

"Shaky," she says, almost to herself.

"So who's my dad?" I ask. No millionaire, that's for sure, I think. Probably some skuzzy dude from East Van. Tattoos, a mullet, bad teeth. I finger my own hair, which has had better days.

"I'm getting to that," she says. "Don't rush me."

Even in the middle of this emotional hurricane, she paces herself.

"I flew out from Calgary to get Donna. That's when this picture was taken. We walked along the seawall, and I asked her about the baby's father. She wouldn't tell me anything. Not then, not ever. She said he knew she was pregnant and he had paid for an abortion, but he had no idea she hadn't gone through with it. She didn't want him to know and that was that. I didn't ask why. I figured she had her reasons. I told her I wanted to keep you, and she said okay—as long as I never told you that she was your mother. She didn't want you to hate her, I guess."

"So why are you telling me now?"

"It was in her suicide note. Her dying wish. 'Tell Emily.' So I have." A small tired smile ghosts across her face. "Funny—she didn't seem to care at all if you ended up hating me."

Chapter Three

For the next three days, I lock myself away in my room and read everything in the box. I prop the photograph against my alarm clock so I can refer to it as I search the annual for clues. I sleep with the pink blanket around my shoulders, and I only come out of my room when Sandra—I refuse to call her Mom anymore—is out. I listen for the sound of the back door closing, and I watch from my bedroom window as she either gets in her car or walks down our street toward the beach. She's still going for a lot of long walks, which suits me fine. Every evening she leaves for a walk right after dinner, and I race downstairs and throw out the dinner she has prepared (and labeled) for me. I raid the freezer and devour microwavable junk. Mini-pizzas, Hot Pockets, Tater Tots. I drink a lot of Pepsi. I never clean up.

Back in my room, I try to make sense of the stuff Donna sent me. The birthday cards are all generic Hallmark garbage inscribed with lame Chicken Soup-y poems. Nothing personal. When I turned fifteen, she wrote, "Tell me, what is it you plan to do with your one wild and precious life?" Weird. It wasn't like she was expecting an answer. The letters from Sandra to Donna are full of strange details about my life. Things I've forgotten, like the time when I was two and she lost me in a department store. Apparently I was obsessed with babies, and my mom found me just as I was leaving the store, trailing behind a woman pushing a baby in a stroller. Some things I remember, like winning the prize for the best English essay in grade seven. Some things I really don't need to know, like the color of my baby poop or how much I cried when my teeth came in.

The annual tells me other things. Donna was in the drama club, she didn't do sports, she was kind of hot (for an eighties chick) and she liked to party. I find one picture of her dressed up as Dorothy in *The Wizard of Oz*. Her hair in pigtails, her boobs busting out of her gingham costume. She's clutching a black puppy and she's laughing—her mouth is wide open. You can almost see her tonsils. Or maybe she's singing. In another picture, at what looks to be a cast party, her eyes are glazed and she's laughing up at an older guy, whom I recognize as the drama teacher, Michael something or other. That's it, other than her grad photo and the brief bio that says "Donna dreams of making her mark on Broadway!" I search for myself in her face but I can't see past her big hair and heavy eyeliner.

I give up and read the letters from K again. There aren't very many and they're full of clichés. Soul mates, red roses, sweet surrender, forbidden love. Ugh! If this K guy really is my dad, I hope his writing skills have improved. And what's the deal with the forbidden love? Maybe K is a woman and Donna was gay, but that doesn't make any sense. I sweep the letters onto the floor and flop back on my bed and stare at the ceiling. I am royally pissed off and seriously confused. So far, all I know is that my mother is my aunt. My aunt was my mother. And nobody knows who my father is. I can't do anything about the first two things, but it's time to do something about the last. I've had enough of my room, this house, my life.

The next morning I get up, have a shower and go downstairs for breakfast. The un-mom is sitting at the kitchen table, drinking coffee and reading the paper. She looks up and smiles when I come into the room. There are deep shadows under her eyes and her skin is blotchy. I look away from her and fill a bowl with cereal.

"Hey, sweetie," she says. "Feeling better?"

I can't believe her. She's acting like nothing happened, like we'll just carry on the way we were. Rage rises in my throat and threatens to exit as a howl. Instead I take a bite of cereal and the howl subsides. I'm going to have to speak to her sometime. Might as well get it over with.

"Yeah," I mutter. "I'm okay, I guess."

"That's good." She hesitates. "We should talk…"

"No," I say, "we shouldn't. You did what you had to do. So did Donna. I get that. Now it's my turn."

"What do you mean? Your turn to what?"

"Nothing," I say. "I just wish I could get away from here. From you."

I mean to hurt her and I can see that I have. Her mouth opens slightly and her eyes flutter. Her breathing slows—long slow inhales, deep exhales. Then she nods and says, "I can see that."

What she can't see is that my heart is pounding. Sweat is trickling between my shoulder blades, and my mouth feels like it's full of cotton balls.

"What's your plan for the day?" she asks, as if it's any old Saturday. Why isn't she more upset? Maybe I'm just playing into her grand plan—to get rid of me.

"Nothing much. I might go to the mall with Vanessa later."

"Okay," she says. "Do you need money?"

"Nope."

"How about a ride to the mall?" Wow, she really wants me out of here.

"I'm good," I say.

"Fine," she says. "I'm going to run some errands. Leave me a note if you go out, okay?"

"Sure," I mumble. As soon as she's out the door, I scribble a note that tells her I'm going to Vancouver and I'll be staying at the Y and not to come after me. I pack as quickly as I can. An hour later I am sitting in the backseat of a cab, going to the bus station. I'm listening to Lily Allen on my iPod and trying to stop shaking. Whatever happens in Vancouver, at least I'm finally doing something with my one wild and precious life.

Chapter Four

The bus is crowded, but I snag the last window seat and turn my back on the aisle. I hope nobody sits next to me. Wouldn't you know, right away someone plops down in the seat beside me. It's a girl, older than me, wearing a pink Tommy Hilfiger sweatshirt with stains on the sleeve and frayed cuffs. Generic jeans. Cheap flip-flops. Drugstore earrings. She smiles at me as if we're old friends and says something, but I can't hear her over my iPod. She has a wide smile and crooked, very white teeth. I turn off my iPod as she leans over me to wave to a woman and a little boy, both flaming redheads, who are standing beside the bus. The little boy is crying and jumping up at the window. She blows him kisses, and then she nudges me.

"Is that your mom?" she says, pointing to a middle-aged woman who is waving at the bus from her car.

"Nope," I say. "My mom's dead."

The girl shoots me a puzzled look, and then she waves at the little boy again as the bus pulls out of the station. She sits back in her seat, closes her eyes and exhales loudly, like a walrus. I pull a book out of my pack and hope that, between the book and the iPod, she'll figure out that I'm not in a chatty mood. I glance over at her and see that she still has her eyes closed, but tears are streaming down her cheeks and she is trembling. I try to ignore it, but after a few minutes I reach over and touch her arm.

"Hey, are you okay?" I say, which is pretty dumb, seeing as how she's sobbing.

To my surprise, she nods and puts her hand over mine. In a couple of minutes she stops crying and opens her eyes and smiles. "Thanks. I needed that. I'm okay now."

I nod and turn back to my book.

"I'm Tina, by the way," she says, sticking out her hand.

"Emily," I reply. I don't shake her hand. I can't believe she doesn't get that I don't want to talk.

"Hi, Emily. Where you heading?"

"Vancouver. To see my dad."

"Yeah? Cool. I'm going to college in Vancouver. Nursing school. Better late than never, right?"

"I guess," I mutter and sneak another look at her. I wonder how old she is and who the redheads are. They don't look anything like Tina. She has long dark-brown hair and eyes the color of caramels.

As if reading my thoughts, she says, "When I was in high school I messed up pretty bad. Drinking, partying all the time. My foster parents kicked me out. I met Janice—the woman at the bus station—at a music festival in Courtenay two summers ago. She took me in and straightened me out and made me finish high school. She really kicked my ass. In a good way. I used to look after Axel, her little boy, when she did night shifts at the bar. She's got a job in an office now and a new boyfriend. It's time for me to move on."

"Where are your mom and dad?" I ask.

"My mom's in Port Hardy, I think. My dad took off years ago. I was in foster care by the time I was three. I lost count of my foster families—I think there were five or maybe six. Some good, some not so good. A few really bad."

"Don't you miss your mom?" I ask.

"Not really," Tina replies. "I never really knew her and, hey, I turned out okay."

She winks at me and I laugh. Even though I have no idea whether I'm going to turn out okay.

"My aunt raised me," I blurt out. "I thought she was my mother. Turns out my mother's a crazy woman who killed herself."

"Harsh," Tina says. Then it all spills out of me. I rant and swear and moan and cry all the way to the ferry terminal. The other bus passengers glare at me, but Tina holds my hand and gives me Kleenex from her vinyl purse. By the time we roll onto the ferry, I am exhausted. She hauls me upstairs to the lounge and brings me weak tea with lots of milk and sugar, just the way I like it. She even finds a washcloth in her pack, wets it with cool water and drapes it over my puffy red eyes.

"Go to sleep," she says. "You'll feel better when you wake up."

I hand her my iPod, which normally I don't lend to anybody. She nods and smiles and says, "Sleep, little sister. I'll watch your stuff."

When I wake up, she's gone. So is my iPod. I fling the washcloth at the back of the seat in front of me. I swear loudly enough to make a woman across the aisle hiss "Language!" at me. I flip her off. As I'm just about to find a ferry worker and demand that a search party be sent out, Tina comes out of the washroom. She plunks herself down next to me. She hands me my iPod and says, "Thanks. I ended up reading your poetry book instead. Hope that's okay. "

I feel hot and ashamed and stupid. I nod and babble something about how much I love poetry and how I'm named after a poet and how I want to be a librarian. When the ferry docks, we get back on the bus. Tina sleeps and I stare out the window all the way into Vancouver. My mom and I go to Vancouver a couple of times a year. We always take the bus because she hates driving in "the big city," so when we get to the bus depot I know where to go to catch a bus downtown and how to find the Y. Tina looks totally lost.

"Where are you staying?" I ask.

"With my cousin," she replies. "He's supposed to meet me here, take me back to his place. I'll stay there until I can find my own place near the college."

There's no way I want to hang around the bus station, but I can't just leave her there. What if the cousin never turns up? What if I have to take her to the Y with me?

"Tom's always late," she says. "He's a busy guy. A real estate agent." We're exchanging cell phone numbers when her cousin arrives in a black suv.

"Jump in," he barks at Tina without offering to help her with her stuff. In a flash, she is gone. As they peel out, she sticks her head out the window. She waves her cell phone and yells, "Call me!"

Chapter Five

When I get to the Y, the woman at the front desk tells me that my mother has called. She paid for my room on her credit card. Wow. She's even willing to pay for me to stay away. My room is small but clean. I am suddenly so tired that I curl up on the bed and sleep for two hours. When I wake up, I go to a sushi place on Robson and then come back to my room and go to sleep again. I keep thinking the un-mom will call me, but my phone is silent. She's probably off celebrating her freedom.

The next day I walk on the seawall, check out the Art Gallery, eat cupcakes and gelato on Denman. All the stuff I usually do with my mom. It's not nearly as much fun alone and it's expensive. I have lots of babysitting money, but I'm going to have to be careful. Vancouver's a pricey place. I don't dare go into the clothing stores on Robson. Usually when we're here, my mom (I can't stop thinking of her that way) buys me one special thing—a pair of shoes, a purse, a skirt. Not gonna happen this time.

The next morning, after breakfast, I head out on the bus to Donna's old school. When I get there it's class change time. I try to blend in and cruise around. I check out the framed photographs that line the halls, thinking how all high schools feel the same. If I weren't feeling so stressed, I'd probably find the old pictures of Sandra funny—debate club, chess club, math club (big surprise). She had huge glasses and crap clothes. Donna is only in the drama club pictures, just like in the annual. No math club for her. She played the lead in lots of productions—*Show Boat, My Fair Lady*. She was even Maria in *The Sound of Music*. I can't find anyone named Ken or Kevin or Kurt or Keith in any of the pictures. I head to the office and look for the oldest woman in the room. There's one in every school office. Someone who's been there forever. Someone who knows where the bodies are buried.

"Yes?" says the woman behind the counter. I can see right away that she's too young to help me. Her hair is frosted and her nails are acrylic.

"I'm doing a paper for my, uh, English class. It's about the history of the drama club, so I, like, need to talk to Mrs., uh, Mrs....you know, the school historian."

"You mean Mrs. Mitchell?" says the woman. "She's hardly the school historian, but she has been here for years."

"Yeah, Mrs. Mitchell. She's supposed to be great." I figure a little sucking up can't hurt.

"You could say that," says the woman with a laugh. She points to a desk by the window. "Wait over there."

A few minutes later a tiny woman scurries back to the desk, gripping a teapot in one hand and a mug in the other. She looks like a mouse. She has brown hair, brown clothes, brown shoes, small darting brown eyes, a twitchy nose.

"Oh, I didn't realize I had a visitor," she says. Even her voice is squeaky. "Tea?" She holds up the pot.

"No thanks. I just need some information for a paper. About the drama club."

She pours her tea and clasps her mug in her tiny pink hands. Now that I have her attention, I don't know what to ask. To buy a little time, I drag the annual out of my pack and plunk it on her desk.

"I'm researching the years between 1988 and 1992, and I'm just wondering if you could tell me about some of the students." I pretend to search for a picture. "Donna Bell, for instance. She was in so many plays." My palms are sweating as I turn the pages. I feel sick to my stomach, the way I feel on the high diving board at the pool.

"Oh, yes, Donna. Darling girl. Very talented. And so pretty. So different from Sandra. It was tragic, what happened to Donna. Such a waste."

I can't tell if Mouse-woman is referring to Donna's death or her pregnancy. I want to defend Sandra for some reason, to tell this old busybody that there's more to life than being pretty and popular. Like being sane, for instance.

"What happened?" I ask.

Mrs. Mitchell leans across the desk and whispers, "She got herself pregnant. Left school. Never came back."

I try to look appropriately shocked. I guess I succeed, because Mrs. M. reaches out and pats my hand and says, "It happens more often than you'd think, my dear, but I'm sure you know that. And I'm sure you're too smart to let it happen to you. Back then, though, girls didn't stay in school when they got pregnant. I heard that Donna gave the baby up for adoption. Probably all for the best." She sighs and folds her hands in her lap. "It certainly left a hole in the drama club. And then Mr. Keene left. It's never been the same, in my opinion."

The expression "the penny dropped" suddenly takes on new meaning. I feel as if a giant piggybank full of pennies is crushing my chest. I struggle to fill my lungs.

"Why did Mr. Keene leave?" I try to speak slowly and calmly but the words come out fast and loud.

Mrs. M. tilts her head to one side and says, "You don't go here, do you, dear?"

"No," I gasp. "I'm the baby. Donna's baby. I'm trying to find my father."

The mouse-woman's bright little eyes close for a moment and when she opens them, she stands up. She smoothes down her skirt, takes me by the hand and leads me out to the hall. We stand in front of a picture of the cast of *Annie Get Your Gun*. Off to one side in the photo is a man in a dark suit. She points at him and says, "Michael Keene. They were always together, he and Donna. He was fired right after she left. Runs a bar called the Bull's Eye, the last I heard. You have a bit of his look about the eyes, dear. He wasn't a bad man. Very smart. Very young. We all liked him." She pats my hand again and says "Good luck" before she scuttles back to the office.

I stand and stare at Michael Keene for a while. He looks ordinary, but the mouse-woman is right. I do look a bit like him about the eyes.

Chapter Six

It's not like I've never been to a bar before, but usually I'm wearing heels and carrying a fake ID. When I get to the Bull's Eye the next day, I'm wearing jeans and a T-shirt that says *My Dashboard Hula Girl Can Beat Up Your Dangling Jesus*. The only other shirt I brought has an Emily Dickinson quote on it—*Forever is composed of nows*. I figure the hula girl one will go over better in a bar. The Bull's Eye is a dive. A dark, narrow, smelly dive. The best thing about it is the neon sign outside—a blue arrow flying over and over into the dead center of a red and white target. Inside there are a few banged-up tables and a long bar. Even though it's only noon, there are guys draped over the bar and lounging at the tables. Every last one of them is smoking, despite the No Smoking signs. As I walk in, they all look up and watch me make my way to the bar. A couple of them offer to buy me a drink. Another one suggests we go back to his place and party. What a self-esteem boost.

"I'm looking for Michael Keene," I say to the guy behind the bar. He is standing with his back to me, washing glasses.

"That's me," he says, turning around and drying his hands. "But I don't serve minors, no matter how cute they are." He grins. I grin back, like an idiot.

He can't be Michael Keene, unless Michael was teaching high school when he was five. This guy can't be more than twenty-four. A very hot twenty-four.

"You're Michael Keene?"

"Yup. Technically, I'm Michael Keene Junior. Call me Mike."

Mike. Junior. No wonder Donna was forbidden fruit. Michael Keene Senior was married. With a kid.

"And you are…?"

"Sandy." I try not to stutter. "Sandy Dickinson. I go to Northwood. I'm doing a paper on the drama club, and Mrs. Mitchell suggested I talk to… your dad."

"Ah yes. Mrs. Mitchell. Dad told me about her. He called her the Mouse. She got my dad fired." Mike frowns and adds, "Well, to be fair, he got himself fired, I guess, but she didn't help. But I'm sure you don't want to hear about that stuff. He was an amazing drama teacher. The best Northwood ever had."

"I'd like to talk to him. Get his stories firsthand, I mean."

"Not possible," Mike says.

"Why—is he out of town?"

"Permanently. He died last year. Car accident. He was in a crosswalk and a drunk driver plowed into him."

I sit down and try not to let him see how freaked out I am.

"Can I have a Pepsi?" I ask. "No ice?"

"Sure," he says. "Coke okay?" When I nod, he continues. "I can try and help you with your paper, though. Or you could talk to my mom. Even though he got fired, Dad loved to talk about Northwood. About all the plays he directed, how some of his students went on to Broadway and movies."

Not all of them, I think. I take a sip of my Coke and watch him wipe the bar. I took an ethics class last year, and I can recognize an ethical problem a mile off. This is definitely a big one. The hot guy behind the bar is my half-brother, but he has no idea who I am. Am I morally obliged to tell him? Or can I just pump him for information about my dad and then split? I must have been silent for a while, because he nudges my elbow and says, "Are we done here? 'Cause if you don't want to talk, I've got stuff to do."

"Sorry," I say. "Can I see a picture of

your dad? That would really help. All I've seen are group photos."

"That's him," he says. He jerks his thumb at a framed black-and-white photograph behind the bar. A professional headshot. It shows a smiling man of about forty. Dark hair, dark eyes—my eyes—slight overbite (thanks, Dad), a tiny scar on his forehead. Mike Junior has the same smile, but he's blond and his teeth are perfect. "He acted around town—little theater groups. Anywhere that was doing a musical. After Northwood, he gave up directing. Said it was too messy, whatever that means. My mom is a teacher too, but little kids. She says one teenager was enough for her." He laughs and asks, "You giving your parents a hard time yet?"

For once I tell the truth. "Not really," I reply. I have never given and never will give my parents a hard time. It's technically impossible.

Mike takes care of bar business while we talk. He's full of stories about his dad, and I try to act like a good little student and scribble away in my notebook. It's obvious that Mike's family went through some rough years after Mike Senior left Northwood, but Mike is vague about the details. I don't really think I can ask, "What about Donna Bell and her baby?" What he is clear about is that his parents worked it out. Whatever "it" was. He also keeps saying what a great guy his dad was and how much he misses him. I want to ask what kind of a great guy knocks up and abandons one of his high school students, but is that fair? According to Donna, he thought she had an abortion. He even paid for it. I wonder what Donna did with the money. I doubt she used it to buy baby clothes.

After three Cokes and an hour of Mike's stories, I have to pee so bad that I risk a trip to the ladies' room, which is surprisingly clean. There's even a hilarious framed poster on the wall. *The Sound of Music* starring Michael Keene as Captain von Trapp. That must have brought back a few memories of the good old days at Northwood High.

When I come out, I gather up my stuff and shake Mike's hand. I promise to send him a copy of my paper and I stumble out into the sunshine. I start to cry as I walk to the bus stop. I cry as the bus crosses the bridge to downtown. I cry when I buy a Starbucks Frappuccino. I cry as I walk back to the Y. People turn away from me as if I'm spraying bird flu germs all over them. I have no Kleenex, so I use my sleeve to mop up the snot. I wish Tina was here with her cool washcloth. When I finally get back to my room, she's the only person I can think of to call, but all I get is her voice mail. I leave a message asking her to meet me tomorrow. Then I climb between the thin sheets and cry myself to sleep.

Chapter Seven

I meet Tina the next afternoon at a café on Robson where a cute barista decorates my latte foam with a wobbly heart. I wish I was more inclined to flirt, but all I can mumble is a lame "Awesome. Thanks" as he lingers by our table.

Tina is wearing the same clothes as before, and there are purple shadows under her eyes. She brushes off my questions about Tom, although she does admit he parties a lot and there's no food in his kitchen. Just a lot of booze.

"The sooner I get my own place, the better," she says, "but everything's so expensive here. I had no idea. I'm probably going to have to live in, I dunno, Surrey. Or find a shared house closer in. It'll work out, though." She sips her undecorated black coffee. I wish I'd thought to order her a latte. She needs a foam heart as much as I do. Maybe more.

"You sounded pretty upset on your message. Did you find your dad?" she asks.

"Sort of," I say. I stab my latte's heart with a wooden stir stick. "He's dead. Which makes me an orphan, I guess. Little Orphan Emily. And no Daddy Warbucks in sight."

"How did you find out that he was dead?"

"His son told me. His very cute son, Mike Junior. My brother. Or half-brother, I should say."

"No way," Tina says. She slams her mug

onto the table and spills the coffee. "You've got a brother. That's great!"

The cute barista zooms over with a rag and mops up the spreading pool of coffee. He must have been keeping an eye on us, which makes me feel both annoyed and pleased. He refills Tina's mug and flashes a dazzling smile in my direction before heading back behind the counter.

"He's flirting with you," Tina says with a giggle. "He's cute. Excellent ass."

"At least he's not related to me," I say. "Mike flirted with me too. It was weird. I almost flirted back. But then I kept thinking how grossed out he'd be when he found out I was his half-sister."

"So you're going to tell him?" Tina asks.

I groan and put my head in my hands. "I don't know. Should I?"

Tina leans over and touches my arm. "You don't have to decide right this minute, you know. He's not going anywhere, right? Tell me about your dad."

So I tell her everything that Mike told

me. That our dad would bust out singing anywhere, anytime. That he made sure the regulars at the Bull's Eye didn't drive drunk. That he always sang "Some Enchanted Evening" to his wife on her birthday. As I talk, it finally sinks in that my father was a real person, not an anonymous sperm-donor. He was a real person who never knew I existed, didn't know what color my baby poop was, how I got lost at the mall, how I won the English prize in seventh grade.

When I finish talking, I'm crying again and Tina is fishing in her purse for more Kleenex.

"He sounds like a good guy," she says as my sniffles subside.

"Who?"

"Your dad, I mean, but Mike too. They both sound like good guys."

"Good guys don't sleep with their students and cheat on their wives," I state.

"Even good guys make mistakes," Tina says gently. "At least you have a bit more information now. You can go home and think about what you want to do with it."

"Go home?" I say. "You think I should go home?"

"Well, yeah," she says, looking surprised. "You have to go home sooner or later. And you did what you came to do. You found your dad. And you need to go back to school too. The longer you stay away, the harder it will be to go back. And you have to go back. You need to talk to Sandra. Hang with your friends."

All of a sudden I am furious with her. She doesn't even know me. I only met her a few days ago. Why am I even asking her what I should do? She has no idea what my life is like. As I stand up to leave, she stands with me and says my name very softly. "Emily."

"What?" I growl.

"Your mom needs you."

"I don't have a mom," I say. I sling my pack over my shoulder. "Remember?"

"We both have mothers," she replies. "They're just not who we want them to be."

"You got that right," I mutter as I stomp out of the café. On the way out, the cute barista hands me a slip of paper. I crumple it up and throw it on the ground. Behind me, Tina bends over to pick it up. She stops and says something to the barista—probably apologizing for my rudeness—and I break into a run. I'm halfway down Robson Street in no time, breathing hard and sweating. Tina is nowhere in sight.

"Smooth move, Emily," I say out loud. I figure there are so many crazies on the street that one more babbling lunatic won't matter. Maybe I'm more like Donna than I thought. Maybe soon I'll be hearing voices telling me to steal a jacket from Banana Republic, but for now all I hear are the noises of the city. And my cell phone, which plays the first few notes of James Brown's "I Feel Good." Which I don't, especially when I look at the display and realize it's the un-mom calling.

I'm not ready to talk to her, and I am not sure that I ever will be. I put the phone back in my pack. I carry on down Robson all the way to Denman and then down Denman to the ocean. Along the way I grab a mango gelato and a chocolate cupcake. Nobody flirts with me, the food tastes too sweet and I am beginning to regret throwing away the cute barista's number. If I stay in Vancouver, I'll need a friend. Even if I only stay one more night. Maybe I could take him back to the Bull's Eye with me. Maybe we could just grab a burger somewhere and chat. Like normal people. Except there's nothing normal about me right now.

I sit on the grass in front of the Sylvia Hotel. I take the picture of Donna and Sandra out of my pack. I hold the photograph in my hand and stare at where they posed for it. It dawns on me that I am in the picture too—invisible but present, already a force in two women's lives. Until this moment, my tears have all been for myself—my loss, my pain, my anger. As I stare at Sandra and Donna, I see for the first time the look of confusion on Donna's face, the expression of love on Sandra's. I see Donna's hand caressing her belly—caressing me. And I see Sandra's arm supporting her sister. Questions whir in my brain like wasps in an empty beer bottle. The hotel isn't about to give me any answers, nor is the photograph, so I take the little pink blanket out of my pack, ball it up into a pillow, lie down and go to sleep.

The next thing I know, I hear a voice say, "Is she dead, Mommy?" and I open my eyes to see a tiny girl in a red dress standing over me.

"Get away from there, Amy," her mother says sharply, as if I'm contagious or something.

Might as well be dead, I think. I gather up my stuff and trudge back to the Y.

Chapter Eight

The next day I get on the bus and go home.
I can't think of anything more to do in
Vancouver, and I'm running out of money
anyway. The woman who sits next to me
on the bus opens a *People* magazine the
minute she sits down. For a second I miss
Tina and her particular brand of nosiness.
I'm starting to worry about all the school
I've missed. Eight days off school in grade
twelve is a lot, and the possibility of not

graduating is truly horrifying. Another year with the un-mom? No way that's gonna happen. I'll just have to work my butt off and get out of there. Maybe Tina and I will share a place in Vancouver. Maybe I'll travel a bit. Maybe I'll take a bartending course and learn how to make drinks with ridiculous names. All I know for sure is that I'll be gone—somewhere.

When I get home, it's dinnertime and Sandra is out. Probably off having a good time with her friends. The really weird thing is that the house is a mess. There are take-out containers everywhere, dirty clothes piled on top of the washer, gunk on the kitchen floor. Sandra hates sticky floors—she says they make her feel like a fly on flypaper. The mess must mean that she's either 1) sick, 2) dead or 3) moved away and rented the house to someone whose housekeeping skills are pretty sketchy.

I unglue myself from the kitchen floor and run upstairs. I'm still mad at her, but I don't want her dead. Not really. The house is going to be a bitch to clean even without a dead body to deal with.

She isn't lying in a pool of her own blood in her bedroom, nor is she passed out in her office or lying in the tub with the toaster, but there are mugs with cold tea in them on almost every surface. They are on the desk beside her computer, on top of the books on the night table, on the windowsills, on the dresser, on the file cabinet, on the back of the toilet. I even find one in the medicine cabinet next to a half-empty bottle of Ativan. When the un-mom is stressed, she drinks tea, lots and lots of tea. She only takes tranquilizers when she has to fly, and she never lets mold grow in her tea mugs. Not that I know of, anyway. But then there are obviously lots of things I don't know about Sandra.

I gather up as many mugs as I can, take them downstairs and start cleaning up the kitchen. I've done two loads of dishes and one load of laundry (my own—I'm not a saint), and I'm just filling a pail with soapy water when the back door opens and Sandra walks in. She doesn't look as if she's been out having a good time. She looks as if she hasn't showered, brushed her hair (or her teeth) or changed her clothes since I went away. She could easily generate some extra income bumming change downtown.

"Emily," she says. "You're back." Her voice is soft, and her eyes look sort of blurry. Maybe it's the drugs. Maybe she's just really tired.

"Yup," I say. "I've missed enough school. I need to graduate if I'm gonna get out of here."

"You do," she says, and I can't tell if it's a statement or a question. "Are you okay?" she asks.

"Better than you," I reply. I put the pail of soapy water down on the kitchen floor. "This place is a sty."

She shrugs and takes off her coat. As she crosses the floor, her muddy shoes leave black marks on the grimy floor.

"It just didn't seem that important," she says. "The cleaning, I mean."

"Yeah, I can see that. You could make penicillin from the crap I found floating in your mugs."

She smiles at me and for a second it feels like old times—me and Mom, kidding around in the kitchen. Except the kitchen is filthy and she's not my mom.

"At least take your shoes off," I say as I wring out the mop.

As she bends down to take off her shoes, I can see that her roots need touching up. I usually do that for her, but when I think about putting my hands in her hair, I want to puke into the sink. I concentrate on washing the floor, changing the water twice, scrubbing away at blobs of jam and what looks like cat shit, even though we don't have a cat.

When I'm done, I take my stuff up to my room and shut the door. The house is silent. The un-mom isn't talking on the phone or watching TV or listening to the radio or banging pots and pans in the kitchen. She's probably doing what I'm doing—lying on her bed with the curtains closed, staring up at the ceiling and wondering what to do next.

After a while I hear the doorbell ring, and after that the TV goes on. I try calling Tina, but her phone's turned off. I'm not ready to talk to Vanessa or Rory. I think about calling Mike Junior, but what would I say? I'm getting pretty hungry, though, and I can't hear the TV anymore, so I sneak downstairs. I find a note on the kitchen table: *Pizza in the fridge—your favorite.* I pull out the box from Uncle Tony's Pizza Patio and take the double cheese, jalapeno and fig pizza into the living room.

When I turn on the light, I see that Sandra is lying on the couch, a ratty old afghan pulled over her head. As I start to leave the room, she mumbles, "Stay, eat your dinner. I'll go up to bed. We'll talk tomorrow."

Dream on, I want to say. We'll talk when I feel like it, which may be never.

"Enjoy your pizza," she says as she stumbles past me.

"Yeah," I reply. I watch *Law and Order*

reruns while I eat. I wish I had someone to talk to, but Tina's phone is still off. I think about going up to the un-mom's room and waking her up and telling her everything, but I don't do it. She doesn't deserve to know about Donna and Michael Keene and Mike Junior. She doesn't deserve to know about Tina. Or about how lonely and confused I am. Or how I'm afraid I'm going to go crazy, like Donna. Sandra's lied to me for seventeen years. Now she's going to find out how it feels.

Chapter Nine

The next morning I go back to school. Everyone assumes I've been sick all this time, and I don't correct them. My body attends every class. I hear my teachers drone on about equations and syntax and global warming. My hand takes notes, my eyes see what's on the board, but I am not there. Or, to be more accurate, I don't know who the girl is that is living in my body.

On my way to math class, I pause

outside the office and look at the framed photographs that line the hall. They look just like the ones at Northwood, except Donna and Sandra aren't in them, of course. I am in a few of last year's pictures: the tennis team, the yearbook staff, the jazz choir. This year Rory and I are co-captains of the tennis team, I'm the editor of the yearbook, and I still sing in the jazz choir, even though I'll never be as good as Vanessa. I look at Mr. McPherson, the choir leader, who is standing next to me in one of the photos. The thought of sleeping with him makes me itch with disgust. The photos need dusting. I reach out and circle my face in the tennis team photo. Once around, then again and again. Three concentric circles. One for me, one for Donna, one for Michael. Bull's-eye. I do it on every picture of me before I go to math class.

At lunchtime I head for the smokers' tree, a huge chestnut that is probably slowly dying from the poisons leaching out of the thousands of cigarette butts that ring its base. I wrote a poem once about a tree that coughs and leaks black sap and eventually dies. Very cheery. None of my friends smoke. Neither do I. The smokers' tree is as good a place as any to hide.

"Hey," says a girl who is crouching under the tree, hands deep in an enormous purse. A cigarette is dangling from her glossy lips. "Gotta light?"

"Sorry, no," I say. "I, uh, don't smoke."

She looks at me as if I'm insane. She calls to a boy who is sauntering across the field to the tree, hands in the pockets of his hoodie.

"Hey, Jared, gotta light?"

A small silver object arcs through the air, and her hand flicks out and snags the lighter. Her reflexes are amazing, like a frog catching a fly. She lights her cigarette and inhales. The tree shudders.

"You're Emily, right?" she asks. "You're in my French class."

I look at her more closely and nod.

"*Je m'appelle Christa*," she says. "*Voulez-vous une cigarette?*"

"No, I don't smoke, " I say again.

"Bien, que voulez-vous?"

What do I want? That's certainly a good question. I shrug and lean against the tree trunk. Jared lights up a cigarette, and he and Christa watch me in silence while they smoke. When the bell rings, they nod at each other and stub out their cigarettes.

"Later," Jared says as they walk away.

"Okay," I reply. I'm sorry to see them go. I don't plan on going home until dinnertime—maybe I could hang out with them. At least they won't pester me with questions, like Vanessa's been doing.

I'm just about to run after them when I notice that not only is the poor tree being poisoned, but it has been slashed and stabbed as well. There are hundreds of initials and words carved into its tender bark, along with hearts, skulls, flowers, lightning bolts, spiders, guns, swastikas and knives. There's even a cow, or maybe it's a horse. I dig in my pack for my nail file and find a bare spot on the far side of the tree, in between a lopsided heart with a crude knife stuck in it and what looks like the word *crank* or *crack*. I carve slowly and carefully. One circle, two circles, three. Bull's-eye. It's hard work, carving with a nail file, but I finish. My file is toast and I've defaced a living thing, but I feel happy for the first time in days. Well, maybe not happy. Maybe just in control.

After school I go to the mall by myself and buy a small Swiss Army knife. When I get to homeroom the next day, I carve a bull's-eye into my desktop and color it in with a red felt pen. By the time I'm finished, my fingers are bleeding and stained, but I find it comforting to trace the three circles while I listen to Mrs. Gates babble about final exams and graduation. Every desk I sit in gets the same treatment, and by the end of the morning I have carved three bull's-eyes and am in serious need of first aid. I meet Jared and Christa at the smokers' tree at noon, and we go to the McDonald's near the school for Big Macs and fries. I draw a little bull's-eye on my tray, but it doesn't give me the same satisfaction as carving.

By the end of the week I have perfected my carved bull's-eye, but I'm running out of wooden surfaces and I'm getting impatient. Carving a bull's-eye takes too long, and you can't carve brick or cement or drywall or do anything on a grand scale. I decide to graduate to spray paint. It smells bad, but it's fast and forgiving. I find a half-used can of black spray paint under the kitchen sink. After a few practice runs on cardboard boxes, I can paint a bull's-eye in less than three minutes with no drips. On Saturday I take the bus to a distant Wal-Mart and buy six cans of spray paint in a color called, appropriately, "Raving Red."

"Art project," I say to the cashier, who stares at me blankly. She mumbles, "Thanks for shopping at Wal-Mart," as she hands me my change. She won't make much of a witness if I ever get busted.

When I get home, Sandra is sitting at the kitchen table, drinking yet another cup of tea and reading a cookbook. She looks a bit better than she did last week. Not that I care.

"Richard and Chris are coming for dinner," she says. "I'm thinking of making this halibut dish. What do you think?" She holds the cookbook up to me and I glance at the picture as I walk past her on my way to my room. It looks amazing. She knows I love halibut.

"Doesn't matter to me," I say. "I won't be here, anyway."

"Oh, honey," she says. "Please stay. Richard and Chris want to see you. They're bringing dessert."

It's going to take more than my favorite fish and a double chocolate mousse cake to get me to sit down for dinner with the un-mom. I have a sudden vision of me and Sandra and Richard and Chris laughing over the dinner table at my last birthday. Tears form in my eyes. I brush them away.

"I've got plans," I say. "Sorry."

She sighs and says, "We'll save you some cake."

"Don't bother," I reply. "I'm on a diet."

Chapter Ten

I paint my first big bull's-eye that night.
It looks amazing on the back wall of a
gas station across town. Cheerful yet
also slightly menacing. I go back the next
afternoon to admire it, but all that remains
is a faint pink shadow. It looks like blood
seeping through a gauze bandage. A guy
in paint-spattered coveralls is slapping
whitewash over my handiwork. "Goddamn
punks," he says when I stop and stare.

"It's gonna take three coats. Reds are the worst."

I want to tell him that a) I'm not a punk and b) it's stupid to cover up a work of art, but I'm not that crazy. Getting arrested isn't part of my plan, so I mumble, "That's really lame," and head home, where I manage to avoid the un-mom by pretending to have killer cramps.

Every evening after dinner, I go out. I lie to Sandra about where I'm going. I'm pretty sure she knows I'm lying, but she never says anything other than *Don't be too late, sweetie.* She's probably as relieved to get away from me as I am to get away from her, but I wish she'd at least fake an interest in what I'm up to. It's not much of a challenge, lying to someone who doesn't care.

After the gas station, I decorate a Dumpster beside a convenience store. The next night I do a wall in an underground parking garage. I'm getting pretty good. I don't get much paint on my clothes, and I wear surgical gloves so I don't have to worry about my hands. I especially like brick walls. The paint doesn't drip and it gives a weird 3-D effect to the circles. As I paint, I chant my little mantra—Circle One Emily, Circle Two Donna, Circle Three Michael. Emily, Donna, Michael. It's surprisingly calming. Or maybe that's the effect of the fumes. Whatever it is, I feel better just hearing the little ball when I shake the can. I love the hiss of the paint coming out of the nozzle. By the time I'm finished I feel almost happy.

Friday night there's a jazz choir practice at school. I actually intend to go, so I don't even need to lie to Sandra. Singing usually makes me feel pretty good, and I figure I could use the boost. I take paint and gloves because just having them in my pack makes me feel better.

The closer I get to the school, the less I feel like singing or hanging out with people who think choosing a grad gown is an important life experience. By the time I get there, all I can think about is the paint can clanking in my pack. I notice, for the first time, that the walls of my school are brick. Beautiful brick painted a very pale peach.

Instead of heading into the gym, I duck around to the back of the building. I find a blank wall next to the garbage bins. I'm in a hurry, so I do without gloves. I figure I can paint a small bull's-eye and still get to choir practice, but the bull's-eye grows and demands company. I paint another and another and another. I'm running out of paint when a car rolls into the parking lot behind me. I'm caught in the headlights—red-handed, literally.

"Hey!" a male voice yells. "What're you doing?"

I'm not about to answer, so I lob the paint can into a garbage bin and take off across the soccer field. Whoever is in the car yells, "*Stop!*"

I race through the park and make it home in record time. Sandra's car is gone, so I'm safe for the moment. Safe and sound and really shaky. I don't think the guy got a good look at me, and besides, it's just paint. Nothing a coat or two of peach paint can't fix.

In the middle of the night, I wake up when someone pounds on our front door. I can hear Sandra talking to somebody and then my door opens. She says, "Emily, get dressed and come downstairs."

I mumble, "What time is it?" and try not to throw up.

"Twelve forty-five," she says. "Downstairs. Now."

I take my time getting dressed. When I get downstairs, Sandra is sitting at the kitchen table with two cops, having coffee. The smell brings another wave of nausea. Or maybe it's the sight of my pack, sitting in the middle of the table.

"Sit down," says one of the cops, a woman with spiky, bleached blond hair. I sit across from Sandra.

"That your pack?" says the other cop, a man.

I nod.

"Want to tell me what you were doing tonight?"

"I went to jazz choir practice."

"I think you did a little more than that,

Emily," says the woman. "Can I see your hands?"

I slowly bring my hands up from my lap and lay them on the blue placemat. There are red speckles all over my hands and wrists.

"We're going to have to get you to bring her to the station, ma'am," the woman cop says to Sandra, who nods.

The station, as in the police station?

"Am I being arrested?" I squeak.

"Kinda looks that way, doesn't it," says the guy as he stands up and heads for the door. "You know what they say—'Don't do the crime...'"

I want to spit on him, but the look on Sandra's face stops me. She doesn't look angry. She looks the way she did when I broke my arm falling out of an apple tree. And when I got the flu so badly that I threw up for three whole days. And when I lost the sack race at the grade five sports day after I'd trained for weeks in the backyard.

On the way to the police station she

asks me one question. "What were you thinking?" I don't know the answer to that, so I don't say anything. I wonder if I'm going to get fingerprinted and whether they'll throw me in a cell. I just want to get this over with so I can go back to sleep—somewhere, anywhere. I feel as tired as Sandra looks.

When we get there, the two cops ask me questions and I answer them truthfully, since I don't see any point in lying. I want a Pepsi in the worst way, but all I get is water. At the end of an hour I have confessed to vandalizing the school (they don't ask about anything else) and my fingerprints have indeed been taken. I sign my statement and the woman cop says, "You can take her home. For now." She smiles and her partner laughs at some inside cop joke. Sandra glares at them. "Someone will be in touch," the cop continues. "Emily's a good candidate for diversion."

"What's diversion?" I ask in the car, thinking it doesn't sound too awful.

Sandra sighs and says, "Don't get your hopes up, Emily. You're not getting away with anything."

That's what she thinks.

Chapter Eleven

Turns out police diversion is a way of keeping first-time juvenile offenders out of the court system, which sounds pretty good to me. Until I hear that the offender (me) has to apologize to the victim face-to-face *and* do community service *and* go for counseling. I wonder if it's too late to go to jail.

"At least we'll get free therapy," Sandra says, cracking a tiny smile. Always the accountant.

We, I think. *We* are going to therapy?

My caseworker is a guy named Jeff with a very heavy Scottish accent.

"Your mother and I have decided that this case requires a public apology, Emily," he says. He sounds like a character from *Brigadoon*. Apparently I'm to stand up at a school assembly and tell everyone I'm sorry I painted bull's-eyes on the school.

"She's not my mother," I say.

Jeff raises an eyebrow at Sandra. She shrugs as if to say, *What did I tell you?*

"Couldn't I just write a letter?" I plead. The thought of apologizing in front of the whole school is terrifying. I'd honestly prefer a cell with an open toilet.

Jeff ignores me and continues. "You can do it any time in the next two weeks. Just let me know so I can be there. You also have to paint out your, uh, artwork and choose your community service from this list." He shoves a piece of paper across the desk.

I shut my eyes, circle my finger in the air three times—Emily, Donna, Michael—and bring it down on the paper. Bull's-eye.

I open my eyes and see that my finger has landed on the words *Faircrest After-School Program—Cleanup* next to a name and a number. I hand the paper back to Jeff, who says, "Faircrest? Good choice."

I stop listening as Sandra and Jeff bond over the details of my community service and "our" therapy. My thoughts are tumbling in my head like socks in a hot dryer. Everyone will laugh at me. I won't have any friends. The kids at the day care will hate me. I won't graduate. I'll get kicked out of my house. I'll end up on the street. I'll start drinking and I'll get depressed. In other words, I'll turn into my mother. My crazy biological mother. Tears well up in my eyes and start to trickle down my cheeks. I feel a hand on my shoulder and Sandra's voice says, "Come on, Emily. We're done for today."

She takes my hand and leads me out of Jeff's office. By the time we get to the car I am doubled over, sobbing uncontrollably. Snot is streaming out of my nose and into my mouth, which is open in a wail. Sandra props me against the car and takes me in her arms, stroking my hair and singing into my ear, "You are my sunshine, my only sunshine." She's as crazy as her sister.

I decide to get the apology out of the way, since it's the thing I'm most worried about. I can't stand feeling sick to my stomach all the time, even though the weight loss that goes along with it is kind of cool. There's a regular assembly every second Wednesday, so I let the principal know that I need a few minutes to make an important announcement. She doesn't ask what it's about, so I assume she already knows. Probably the whole school knows. I only hang out with Jared and Christa now anyway—all my old friends are keeping their distance, maybe because I never return their calls.

On Wednesday I throw up three times before the assembly—or, to be more accurate, I retch three times, since there's no food in my stomach. When Ms. Appleton calls me out onto the stage, I can see Sandra and Jeff in the front row beside Richard and Chris. They are all smiling encouragingly, as if I'm about to play a violin solo or give a speech about helping the homeless. A little farther back, a tiny hand waves and I see Christa and Jared, who never come to assemblies. I feel weirdly honored.

I clear my throat and say, "My name is Emily Bell. I painted bull's-eyes on the back wall of the school and I'm very sorry." That's all I mean to say, but my mouth starts to move again. "I'm also going for therapy and doing community service and painting over the bull's-eyes. I know there's lots of rumors flying around, so here's the truth: I'm not going to jail and I'm not quitting school and I'm sorry if I hurt anybody."

I look down at Sandra and she's smiling at me and suddenly everyone is clapping and cheering and stomping their feet, as if I'd just announced that there would be free beer at school dances.

Painting over my bull's-eyes turns out to be almost as much fun as doing them in the first place. I have to buy the paint and brushes with my own money, and I find out that what the guy at the gas station said is true—red is a bitch to cover. But the whole thing is a totally backward Tom Sawyer experience—everyone wants to help, and I have to tell them that they can't. So they hang out and talk to me while I paint and bring me Pepsi and Reese's Pieces. Vanessa loads my iPod with new tunes, and Rory brings his speakers. Jared arrives with brownies that he says he made himself (who knew?), and Christa promises to give me a manicure and pedicure when I'm finished. Three coats and three days later, I'm done. The bull's-eyes have disappeared. Ms. Appleton inspects my work and pronounces it excellent.

After dinner that night I tell Sandra I'm going upstairs to work on a school project. In my room I write three letters of apology: I address one to the company that owns the Dumpster, one to the gas station and one to the people who run the parking garage. Inside each envelope is money for enough paint to cover my art and to pay someone to do the painting. I don't sign any of the letters. I'm not crazy. Not yet, anyway. What I am is officially broke.

On Monday I meet the therapist, whose name is Dr. Byron Handel. Sandra comes with me and we set up a schedule. I'll go once a week and Sandra will join us once a month, which is a lot better than having her there every time. Dr. Handel doesn't do much on the first visit other than ask me whether I understand the terms of my diversion and whether I'm willing to, as he puts it, give therapy my best shot. I nod and am surprised to find I mean it.

Tuesday after school I take the bus over to Faircrest Elementary. As I walk up to the door that says *After-School Care*, a woman comes out and asks me if I'm Emily Bell. When I nod, a little girl with straight red hair barrels out the door, screeches to a halt in front of me and sticks out her hand. "I'm April," she says. "Who are you?"

"That's a very good question," I reply as I shake her grubby little hand.

Chapter Twelve

Twice a week I go to the after-school program, where I prepare snacks, wash dishes, wipe runny noses, sweep the floors and tidy up the toys the kids leave lying around.

My partner in all these activities is April Cummings, who attaches herself to me like a limpet. A very chatty limpet. Most days, if I get all my other jobs done, I help her with her schoolwork. If we have time before her mom picks her up, we bake in the center's tiny kitchen. April stands on a chair beside me at the counter, hands me ingredients and keeps up a running commentary—in song. "First we melt the chocolate, the chocolate, the chocolate," she sings as we make brownies. "Then we add the sugar, the sugar, the sugar." By the time the brownies are ready to go into the oven, April is covered in flour and chocolate and I am in hysterics. Her songs are so silly, yet they make me unreasonably happy.

The first day we bake together, April peers suspiciously at the electric mixer and says, "What's that?"

"A mixer—you know, for the cookie dough."

"Oh. We don't have one."

"How do you make cookies then?" I ask, scraping the sides of the bowl.

"We don't make cookies," April says. "We buy them. In really big yellow bags. And my dad gets all the ones with chips in them."

"These'll be better," I tell her, "and you can have the ones with the most chips."

Her green eyes bug out and she starts to hum and then to sing a chocolate chip cookie song. She's heavily influenced by Raffi, but that's okay. Most musicians are sampling someone.

My therapy isn't as much fun as my community service. Dr. Handel doesn't entertain me with silly songs, and I have to talk about myself, which I hate. He's a patient guy, though, and pretty smart. He waits me out, even on the days when I lie down on his couch (yes, there really is a couch) and announce that I have nothing to say. He asks me a couple of innocuous questions and suddenly I can't shut up. The next thing I know he's pointing at his dumb Fritz the Cat clock and telling me our time is up.

I'm not sure what happens in therapy—I don't think anyone, even therapists, knows for sure—but I don't feel as confused and angry and hurt as I did when I first found out about Donna. I'm still pissed at Sandra for lying to me, but I'm beginning to think she didn't have much choice. I don't tell her that, though. I'm not that evolved.

By November, life has settled into a comforting rhythm. Two afternoons a week at the day-care center, one session a week with Dr. Handel. As long as there are few disruptions to my routine, I feel okay. Not fabulous, but okay. I'm like a baby who thrives on regular mealtimes, strict naptimes, familiar faces. I go to jazz choir and I study and I start eating the meals Sandra prepares. I have dinner at Duck Soup with Richard and Chris and Sandra. I call Tina every weekend and tell her how my week has gone, and she tells me about nursing school and her crazy roommates. I invite her for Christmas without asking Sandra if it's okay. I know it will be.

One day in late November, April and I are making gingerbread and she asks me, "Where's your daddy?"

I blink and tell her the truth. "He's dead."

She stops stirring and says, "I wish my daddy was dead too."

"What?" I say, momentarily stunned.

She's only seven. I stare at her, but she looks the same as always: red hair, green eyes, small scar on her cheek, scabby knees, dirty fingernails. "Why?" I stutter, but it's too late. She's started a gingerbread song with about eighteen verses. The next time she mentions her dad is the following week, when she tells me he ate all the gingerbread she took home the week before. Maybe she wants him dead because he eats all the good stuff.

One afternoon we're playing Snakes and Ladders and I notice a small burn on her wrist. She sees me staring and pulls her sleeve down, knocks the board over, bursts into tears and hides her head under a throw pillow. I roll her sleeve up and find three more little round burns on her arm. Cigarette burns.

I pull her sleeve back down and stroke her leg and sing, "You are my sunshine, my only sunshine." After a while she stops crying and her head pops out from under the pillow and she says, "Can I have some cake?"

Every time I see April after that, I check her out for burns or bruises. On the sly, of course. Most of the time I find them. When I ask her where they come from, she says she fell down or Matthew, her little brother, kicked her or she was helping her mom make toast. When her mom comes to pick her up (she's always the last parent to arrive), she doesn't even shut the engine off. She just honks and waits in her car, smoking and listening to Aerosmith. She lets April ride in the front seat without a seat belt. I was, like, ten before Sandra let me ride in front, and she still won't start the car until my seat belt is done up.

After a while, I can't take any more. I have nightmares that one day April won't be at the after-school program, that she will end up in the hospital or, worse, in the morgue. I have seen enough bruises on her pale skin to believe that she is in danger from the very people who are supposed to protect her. It's all kinds of wrong, and I have to tell somebody or I'm going to get violent myself. I've watched enough TV to know I need proof. All I have are suspicions, but I don't know where to take them. I start with Dr. Handel.

"Cigarette burns," he says. "You're sure?" He puts his notepad down and leans toward me. I'm sitting on the edge of the couch instead of lying down like I usually do. April's problems seem so much bigger than mine right now.

"Yup," I say. I pull my own sleeve up to show him a burn on my forearm. "I bummed a cigarette off Jared and burned myself, just to be sure. It hurt like you wouldn't believe." My eyes fill with tears, and I feel a surge of anger so strong it threatens to choke me. "How can anyone do that to a kid? She's only seven. She sings dumb songs while we bake. She cheats at Snakes and Ladders. She makes me laugh. They don't deserve her. She'd be better off with me."

Dr. Handel nods. "That's probably true, Emily," he says. "But you're only seventeen." He pauses. "Have you told anyone? Your mom, maybe, or someone at the school?"

I start to say what I usually say—that she's not my mom—but this time I stop and simply answer, "No."

Chapter Thirteen

I stand in the doorway of Sandra's office. "I need your help," I say.

Sandra looks up from her work. She lowers her glasses and gestures to the client chair.

"Okay," she says. "Shoot."

I take a deep breath. "It's about April," I begin. "I think…I mean…she needs…"

Sandra leans forward. "Go on," she says gently. I continue.

"Someone's hurting her, someone at her house. Dr. Handel says I need to report it, but I..." My eyes fill with tears. Sandra gets up and crouches by the chair and holds me as I cry.

"Dr. Handel says I can call the cops or the ministry or the Kids' Help Line. He says social workers will talk to me and to April, and doctors will examine her, and she'll probably get taken away from her parents. I'm scared. I mean, what if she gets sent to a bad foster home, like Tina did? What if her dad comes after her or something? What if he comes after me?"

Sandra stiffens and stands up. She looks like she did when she caught Billy Conklin burning a cat's tail with a cigarette lighter. Like a mother bear having a very bad day. "What do you need me to do?" she asks.

I had my speech all planned out, but now my tongue feels thick and my lips are glued together. I can't get the words out.

"Emily? Honey? Would it help if April could come here for a while?"

I am still speechless, but for different

reasons. How did she know what I was going to say? And why is she being so generous after all I've put her through?

I nod. "Dr. Handel says that if you talk to the social workers and they see what kind of a..." I pause. "...What kind of a mother you are, and what kind of a home we have, then maybe she can stay with us instead of going to strangers."

"Okay, then," she says. "Let's get that first phone call over with. We'll take it from there."

She sits with me while I call the Kids' Help Line. The woman I talk to is calm and kind, and she makes me feel better about what I'm doing. She tells me what will happen next, to April and to me. Then she talks to Sandra, who takes lots of notes. When Sandra gets off the phone, she leads me up to the kitchen. She sits me down at the table while she makes macaroni and cheese from the box. We sit down to our bowls of bright orange goop, and she takes a bite and says, "Heaven."

I mix ketchup in with mine and I say what I always say. "Sunset in a bowl."

She laughs, as she always does.

The next few days are a blur of interviews and meetings and more interviews and more meetings. Sandra drives me to every appointment and waits for me, sometimes for as long as two hours. She brings her laptop and sits in hallways and drinks a lot of tea. She is also interviewed to see if she's a suitable foster mother for April

It makes me want to scream—how long it takes and how many different people we have to talk to—but one morning, about a week after I made the call, a social worker brings April to our house. Her father has been charged with assault, and her mother has gone into rehab for her drinking. April will stay with us indefinitely. Mom won't get paid right away, but she says that's okay—April's happiness is more important.

I don't expect April to be happy, exactly, but for the first few days she hardly talks to me. She cries all the time and wants her mother. I try to coax a smile out of her by making up songs about macaroons and date squares, but she's not buying it. The social workers have warned me that the transition will be difficult for her, so I try to use what Sandra says is the number one parenting skill of all time: patience

Little by little, April starts to talk about what happened to her after I made the call. She tells me how the doctors poked and prodded her, how the social workers asked endless questions and the police came and took away her dad. She never talks about what her parents did to her. I don't push her to give me details—she's in a state of shock and she misses her home and her little brother and her parents. Her loyalty to the people who abuse her blows me away. I try to go with her to all her appointments, and if I can't go, Sandra goes. There are therapists and more social workers, lots of different ones. Later on there will be court dates and supervised visits with her mom when she gets out of rehab.

But right now we do lots of regular everyday stuff. I take her to school and pick her up. We do our homework together and help Sandra with dinner. We play games and watch TV and paint our toenails crazy colors. I read all my old favorites to her at bedtime—*Goodnight Moon*, *Babar*, *Madeleine*. Once a week I take her to visit her little brother, Matthew, at his foster home. She's a great big sister, loving and careful—the way I am trying to be with her. How an abused seven-year-old knows how to do this is beyond me, and I wonder if Matthew realizes how lucky he is. She is always sad when we have to leave.

After April goes to bed, I usually sit and drink tea with Sandra for a little while before I study or go out with friends. Mostly we talk about ordinary stuff—how April is doing or which exams I'm stressing about or whether we should get a cat. Sometimes we talk about what happened between us. Mostly I'm doing what Dr. Handel suggested—I'm sitting with it, processing the fact that both my biological parents are dead, and while Sandra is biologically my aunt, she really is my mother. I'm not angry about it anymore, and I've gone back to thinking of Donna as my aunt. And Michael Keene Senior? Well, he really was just a sperm-donor after all.

Tina is coming for Christmas. Then we're going to drive her back to Vancouver and we're all going to stay at the Sylvia for a few days. We'll take April to Stanley Park and the Planetarium and go shopping on Robson and eat cupcakes and gelato on Denman. Tina and I will go back to the café on Robson so I can flirt with the cute barista. I'm pretty sure that I'm going to visit Mike Junior and tell him who I am. It scares me, mostly because I don't want to mess up his life, but I think he deserves to know that he has a sister, even a slightly crazy one. I'm going to tell him about the bull's-eyes. I want him to meet Tina and April and Sandra too, but that may have to wait. In the meantime, I've got lots to keep me busy. And happy. That's the most surprising thing. The happiness.

One night after April's bedtime ritual (three stories, a cuddle and a kiss, the bedbug rhyme, lights out), her whisper follows me to the door.

"Are you my sister now, Emily?"

I don't have to give it even a moment's thought. "Sure looks that way, doesn't it?" I reply, smiling in the dark.

"Even if I go back to live with Mommy?" Her little voice is quavering. I flip the light on again and sit on the side of her bed. I look down at her worried little face.

"Here's the way it works," I say, stroking her hair away from her face. "No matter where you go and what you do, we'll always be sisters. Deal?"

"Deal," she says as her thumb rises to her mouth and her eyes close.

"Deal," I say again as I turn out the light and leave the room.

Sarah N. Harvey is an editor and the author of *Puppies on Board*, a picturebook. *Bull's Eye,* her first Soundings novel, was written between Ping-Pong games. Sarah lives in Victoria, British Columbia.

Orca Soundings

Orca Soundings

Visit www.orcabook.com for all Orca titles.

Orca Currents

Orca Currents

Mirror Image
K.L. Denman

Pigboy
Vicki Grant

Queen of the Toilet Bowl
Frieda Wishinsky

Rebel's Tag
K.L. Denman

See No Evil
Diane Young

Sewer Rats
Sigmund Brouwer

Spoiled Rotten
Dayle Campbell Gaetz

Sudden Impact
Lesley Choyce

Swiped
Michele Martin Bossley

Wired
Sigmund Brouwer

Visit www.orcabook.com for all Orca titles.